The Sky Sheriff

The Pioneer Spirit Lives Again in the Texas Airplane Patrol

Thomson Burtis

Pharos Books

ISBN: 978-93-67001-48-6
eISBN: 978-93-59835-54-9

©Publishers

Publisher: Pharos Books (P) Ltd.
Plot No.-63, First Floor, Main Mother Dairy Road
Pandav Nagar, East Delhi-110092
Phone: +14049995474, 011-40395855
WhatsApp: +91 9319228272
E-mail: sales@pharosbooks.in
Website: www.pharosbooks.in
Edition: 2024

Printed By: Sushma Book Binding House, Okhla Industrial Area, Phase II, New Delhi-110020

**The Sky Sheriff : The Pioneer Spirit Lives Again
in the Texas Airplane Patrol**
By : Thomson Burtis

The Sky Sheriff

The Pioneer Spirit Lives Again in the Texas Airplane Patrol

*Sure enough, there was a mounted man
crossing a tiny clearing, two or three miles to the westward*

The blazing sun of a Texas afternoon turned air and drab brown earth to gold. Not a breath stirred the huge white stocking that served as a wind-indicator on the airdrome of the McMullen Flight of the Air Service border patrol.

Seven men were standing in a line south of the airdrome. Six of them were tanned young chaps with the look of the open in their steady eyes with tiny sun-crinkles at the corners. The other man wore a flowing gray mustache, a sombrero that dwarfed the others' Stetsons, and ornately embossed cowboy boots. He was known from one end of the Rio Grande to the other as Sheriff Bill Trowbridge.

A low drone came to the ears of the group, and far in the distance they glimpsed the tiny form of a ship, diving with motor on for the airdrome. Hickman looked up at the plane.

"Probably Tex MacDowell and Sleepy Spears."

"Who's Spears?" asked Trowbridge.

"New man from the Air Service Mechanics' School at Donovan Field," explained Perkins. "He's the sleepiest-looking guy in the world. Yesterday Tex and Sleepy announced they were going to fly to Laredo, if I'd let 'em, and go over to the 'Bee' hangout in Nuevo Laredo, and either win a fortune or else get entirely broke."

Captain Perkins's face was serious.

Sheriff Trowbridge glanced at him sharply. Apparently there was somewhat of puzzlement, disapproval, in the new commanding officer's words.

Trowbridge was grinning widely. "Did yuh ever have any previous experience handlin' wildcats?"

Captain Perkins shook his head. "Live and learn, I guess," said he.

The ship circled northward, banked around toward the field, and the roaring motor ceased. Then the De Haviland dropped over the low fence that formed the northern boundary of the field. Waiting mechanics in front of a hangar seized the wings and helped bring the ship into the line.

The two flyers climbed out of the cock-pits.

"See that short fellow walking as if every step would be his last?" said Jennings. "That's Sleepy."

Trowbridge smote his thigh.

"I get yuh now," he stated. "Isn't Sleepy the hombre that had a run-in with some would-be bad men up in Barnes City a few months ago?"

"He's the one," said Pop Cravath, wiping the sweat from his bald spot with a voluminous khaki handkerchief.

Spears' drooping eyelids were raised to look at the little group. A slow smile stretched the already wide mouth.

"Meet Sheriff Trowbridge, Sleepy," said Perkins.

"Delighted. I've heard several mouthfuls about you, Sheriff," said Sleepy.

"Did you break the 'Bee'?" inquired Trowbridge solemnly.

"They took advantage of us," sighed Sleepy. "They fed us Benedictine and Mescal. The last I remember was shooting two hundred at the crap-table and then bursting into ribald grief when two sixes turned up. We woke up in the alley alongside the Laredo House this morning."

Captain Perkins's lean, square-jawed face was crossed with varying expressions of merriment, wonder, and disapproval. Apparently the Captain was completely puzzled—unable to understand the facets in his flyers' characters.

"I've got to meet the four-ten from San Antone," said the Sheriff, suddenly. "My old friend George Bilney is comin' in. Say, I'm going to bring George out here this evenin', mebbe. He's station agent and storekeeper up here at Willett. He's only in town to the back train at ten, but he's got a daughter you boys ought to meet. She's the Queen of Sheba, and likewise the Lily of the Valley."

"That sure is interesting. You show us a way to meet her, Sheriff, and we'll show ourselves grateful," said Sleepy.

That evening Sleepy Spears drove a dusty roadster down the main street of McMullen. He saw the train come in and saw the sheriff meet Pappy George Bilney, a little wisp of a white-bearded man.

Sleepy then drew up to the curb in front of a drug store with a flourish and shut off the motor. As he turned to climb out, his gaze fell on the face of a tall, thin, stooping fellow with drooping brown mustachios. As if by some hypnotic influence, the stranger's close-set eyes rose to meet the flyer's gaze, then dropped. The man walked on.

"That's that foreman from Barnes City!" murmured Sleepy. "Must 'ave just got out of jail, if old man Shaler did what he said he was going to do after this bird's scheme to tar and feather poor old Correll. I wonder what he might be doing here?"

A like mental query regarding Spears was arousing fear in the mind of the "bird"—Cal Buchanan, as he called himself. For Cal Buchanan, being a coyote by nature instead of a wolf, had within the last few hours formulated a wolf's plan to resuscitate his fallen fortunes, and when a coyote essays a wolf's role he is likely to shy at a shadow.

As he lounged along the lively street, his small eyes roved constantly, seeing nothing but mental images. Girls and women whose clothes would not have been out of place on the leading thoroughfares of the largest cities; trimly dressed men along with others in cowboy boots and flannel shirts; here a store window that might have been transplanted from Manhattan next to a display of ornate saddles and lariats; a five-thousand-dollar limousine passing a hitching-rack where drooping cow-ponies awaited their owners—all were vague to him as he remained immersed in his plans.

Sleepy Spears had been farthest from his thoughts until the square, sunburnt countenance had appeared with all the effect of a sudden and unwelcome vision.

His thoughts turned back to his experience with Spears six months before. While drunk, he had visited the Barnes City fair, where Spears and Al Johnson, from Donovan Field, were giving flying exhibitions. Then had come that row with Correll, Spears's mechanic, and the dream of tar-and-feathering Correll with the help of three confederates.

In a remote cabin the plan was working well, and the four men were just ready to strip Correll, when a human tornado in the form of Spears had burst in the door. From that time on, events were rather vague in Buchanan's mind. Later he had learned that Spears, learning of the plot too late to overtake the hazing party by automobile, had made a parachute jump at night from Al Johnson's airplane in order to reach Correll in time.

Was there any possibility that Spears, recognizing him, could interfere with the scheme that he had in mind? Nervous as a cat, he finally arose, leaving his food, paid his check, and walked out. Spears or no Spears, his mind was made up. There did not seem to be any reason to believe that the flyer could possibly get on to the scheme he had in mind. And he was desperate.

Six months in the Barnes City jail had been his sentence for the attempted tar-and-feather soirée, At the expiration of his term, three days before, he had been left under no misapprehension as to whether his room was preferable to his company in Barnes City. He had drifted aimlessly toward the border, with vague plans of going into Mexico. A hundred dollars was his capital, and to his craven heart the future loomed dark—until that spry little old man, Bilney, who had boarded the train at Willett, made friends with him, and gave him an opportunity to recuperate his fortunes.

George Bilney had prattled proudly during the whole seventy-five-mile trip from Willett. He kept a general store at Willett, though it was only a tiny station and his nearest customers lived six miles away. His main source of profit, however, was his ranch business. Six ranches, ranging from six to fifty thousand acres, did all their business with him, because of the convenience of having him do the buying, and because he kept a large and assorted stock from which a hurry call for anything from tools to feed or worm-salve could always be filled. Warehouses full of feed, tools, wire, lumber, provisions, and all the other supplies necessary for the modern ranch testified to the volume of his business. As a matter of fact, his store and its other buildings actually formed the so-called town of Willett.

His daughter, home for her college vacation, his dead wife, his boyhood in New England—the little storekeeper had told it all to the sympathetic Buchanan, and among all the details one other thing, which had set that coyote's heart to thumping as he heard it. For it appeared that most of the customers of the store paid their bills on the last day of the month—"It takes quick turnovers for cash to run my business," Bilney had said. And the money was not sent to McMullen until the next morning, on the one daily train that ran south.

Bilney had said that he was returning on the ten o'clock train that evening. Buchanan could slip into a berth, ride to the next station north of Willett, which was twenty-five miles, hire a horse, and ride back in the evening of the next day. Bilney had given him a cordial invitation to drop in for a meal at any time.

It would be absurdly simple. If the money was in a safe, he could force the old man to open it; then bind up him and his daughter, cut the telephone wires, perhaps leave a note on the front of the store saying that the owner would not be back until next day, to give him twelve hours' respite. In that time, by hard riding on the excellent saddle-horse that Bilney had bought for his daughter, Buchanan could make the border. Then for an easy life in Mexico.

Bilney, on the next evening, was reading the San Antonio Express by the light of a big white-shaded kerosene lamp, while Cissy, the huge negro woman who was his housekeeper, prepared supper. On the other side of the table a tall girl with a mass of black hair and a sweet face, was fondling a bull-terrier puppy.

Buchanan paused outside the window and took in the scene. The old man lived in the rear of his store, which was now closed, so Buchanan knocked on the back door.

Bilney opened it, and for a moment peered nearsightedly through his glasses, set half-way down his nose.

"Well, well, come right in, my boy. How did you get up here so quick?" he said.

"I got me a job at the Blackburne ranch to-day, and I just thought I'd drop in t' say howdy," returned Buchanan, entering hesitantly.

"Glad to see you. Company's scarce around here. Meet my daughter Judith—Cal Buchanan, Judith."

Judith's voice had the musical slowness of the South. Bilney set out cigars. Buchanan, ill at ease and in a nervous tremor, refused both and talked infrequently. He found it hard to meet the tranquil eyes of the girl; he devoted most of his attention to her father, who talked enough for all three.

The little sitting-room was cozy and homelike in the soft light of the lamp. The flat tints of the wall and the selection of prints and furniture showed a taste that gave subtle individuality to the room. Without knowing the exact reason for it, his surroundings increased Buchanan's discomfort.

Supper—Judith called it dinner—was an ordeal. Bilney wore a coat over his flannel shirt and black bow-tie, and Judith's white frock contrasted with Buchanan's dirty vest and flannel shirt, open at the scrawny neck. A snowy table-cloth, simple silverware—all were foreign to his usual surroundings. Finally Judith succeeded in drawing some halting conversation from him on the subject of horses. She was a typical Texas girl in her love of riding. Occasionally he felt her large eyes resting on him, and felt the goose-flesh start on his body. Somehow or other, she seemed a bigger obstacle to him than her spry little father. The negress added to the complications somewhat, but not too greatly. He strove to steady himself by thinking of what the successful culmination of his enterprise would mean to him.

The meal over, he sat in the sitting-room hour after hour, unable to launch his offensive. When Bilney insisted on his spending the night with them, he accepted like a drowning man grasping at a plank. He forgot the value of time as he convinced himself that with the household asleep he would have greater chances for success.

At ten-thirty Buchanan huskily announced his desire for sleep. His host showed him his room, which opened off the sitting-room, as did his own room and Judith's. The store was reached through a passage from the living-room, which skirted the store office and opened directly into the passageway between two counters. His last mental picture was that of Judith kissing her father good night.

Without undressing, he threw himself across the spotless white spread and stared at the ceiling. Through the open window came the drone of myriad insects, and the almost inaudible scratch of hundreds of them up and down the screen. The slight gulf breeze ruffled the mesquit trees outside, and occasionally the yelp of a coyote came to his ears.

How long he had waited he did not know; but when he finally removed his boots and stole out into the dark living-room, lamp in hand, it seemed as if an eternity had passed. He meant to reconnoiter a bit. With all the yellow heart of him he hoped that he might get the money and go without the necessity of binding Bilney and the two women, or of compelling the old man to tell him where the money was.

With a hand that shook so that the chimney rattled, he set the lamp down on the battered table in the office.

He drew a pair of cutters from his shirt and quickly snipped the telephone wires. The snap of a board beneath his feet nearly caused him to drop the tool.

This accomplished, his small eyes darted around swiftly. The table, a closed roll-top desk with a battered swivel-chair, and a heap of old pasteboard boxes and circulars in a corner of the tiny room represented the only furnishings. Apparently there was no safe.

He tiptoed to the window and pulled the wrinkled green shade to the bottom. He tried the top of the desk, and it rolled up obediently. Within was a small metal box, locked with a hasp and a small padlock.

He gasped with relief. His first impulse was to grab the strong-box and run. With an effort he resisted the temptation. He must make sure that the money was there.

He wiped his moist palms on his overalls, and vainly tried to control the tremors that shook him. He took out the heavy cutters, with the idea of using them as a lever in an attempt to break the box. He was just starting to insert them below the hasp when padding footsteps came to his ears.

An exclamation that was like a sob burst from his ashen lips as he turned, his fingers gripped around the instrument in his hands. Dim against the blackness of the open door, because of the lamp between, he saw the scraggly white hair and peering eyes of Bilney. A trembling revolver flashed close to the door-jamb.

Blindly, unthinkingly, Buchanan leaped forward and swung. He was in an ecstasy of terror. The report of the wild shot echoed like thunder an instant before his weapon sank in the skull of the trembling old man. He dropped, limply horrible. The revolver crashed to the floor.

"Daddy!"

Swiftly flying footsteps up the passage came to his ears like the approach of some avenging fate. He met the girl as she burst through the doorway. His hand closed over her mouth. Her anguished eyes blazed into his.

*He met the girl as she burst through the doorway,
her anguished eyes blazed into his and for a moment
she seemed petrified with terror.*

He was conscious, through his trance of fear and horror, of screams rising eerily through the night. He took his hand from her mouth long enough to rip out her silken sleeve, stuff it into her mouth, and bind it there with his bandana.

She came to herself then, and fought like a wildcat as he tried to bind her hands and feet. It was half a minute before he succeeded.

He did not wait to bind her feet, but hurried back toward those screams, careless of the blackness of the passageway. He ran into the table in the dining-room, and blundered toward the kitchen. The screams rose in a crescendo of utter terror as he approached.

Moonlight filtered through the windows of the tiny bedroom, and by its dim illumination he could see the whites of staring eyes in the corner behind the bed. He jerked the gibbering old negro to her feet and his fist crashed to her jaw. He ripped and tore at the bed-sheets like a wild man, finally securing strips that answered for a gag and strands to secure arms and legs.

He ran back to the office, to fall over the prone body of the old man. He rolled away from it as if from some living menace. He scrambled to his feet, his breath coming in labored gasps, and turned toward Judith, whom he had flung in the chair before the desk. She was limp, her face still set in lines that seemed frozen in agony. He finished his task of binding her.

With the cash-box in his arms, Buchanan fled. It was the work of a moment to enter the small corral, fling the saddle that hung in the shed on the back of Judith's saddle-horse, and mount.

The whispering mesquit was the voice of phantom pursuers, the solitude terrible.

He galloped to the little shack depot, and let himself in by smashing a window. The moon-rays through a window gave enough light to enable him to smash the telegraph instruments and the telephone.

Then, without food or water, he set off at a wild gallop southward. His convulsed face was twisted backward over his shoulder as if he expected the blurred buildings behind him to give forth some avenger to follow him through the shadows reaching for him from every side.

Captain Perkins was sprawled in the swinging hammock on the porch of the recreation building, puffing deliberately at a short pipe. It was a little after ten o'clock in the evening. Presently the sheriff happened along.

The lean-faced, square-jawed commanding officer was wrestling with some of the problems that his new detail had brought him. Transferred from the engineers a few months before, he had found that flyers bore little resemblance to the correct young West Pointers he had known in the infantry and the engineers. And his first detail as a commanding officer, he admitted frankly to himself, had him guessing.

"I ain't been around the border cavalry since Washington crossed the Delaware for nothin'," the Sheriff advised him. "Cap'n, in my judgment, you got to figger this here Air Service as different from any other. Course, I may be jest a foolish old-timer which ought to o' passed out quiet and decent a matter o' ten years ago, but this here bunch o' yours, and the other boys from down Laredo and Marfa way that I run into, have kinda sneaked under my hide. By and large, the idee o' these planes spannin' the border from California to the Gulf o' Mexico, risin' out o' little cleared spots in the Big Bend and out there in Arizona, and these boys flyin' 'em over them El Paso mountains and the deserts and this Godforsaken strip of mesquit, riskin' their lives every minute they're in the air—it's kind o' doggone romantic to even an old sand-rat like me.

"And rememberin' the times when fellers like Sam Edwards, which is now fat and a mayor and washes his neck regular, was r'arin' youngsters ridin' down main streets drunk and shootin', and rememberin' what true-blue buddies and real hombres they was, makes me judge your boys in the same class.

"And listen, son: the old days in this country meant that a man had to have guts or go under. Because they was men ridin' the range and maintainin' their necks as good as new by their own gun-play, the same red blood which showed in them things was responsible for what's known now as the old 'wild West' stuff.

"I reckon your boys are pioneers, Cap'n. To my notion, any man that picks this here flyin' as a profession ain't ever goin' to get no kick out of a ten-cent-limit poker game. Where would yore Air Service be if the men in it was playin' things safe?"

He raised his voice at the last words, for the brooding silence of the night was shattered by the rolling explosions of a motor.

Spear's battered roadster shot down the road, its huge headlights probing the darkness. It swooped around the sharp corner with breath-taking speed, stopped with startling celerity, and died into silence. The flyer strolled toward the porch, peering briefly at the two occupants thereof.

"Hello," he greeted them briefly, as he sank on the steps. "I want to inquire about the ringleader of that Barnes City tar-and-feather party I saw get off the train yesterday afternoon. Tall, hungry-looking guy with a long mustache."

"Name o' Buchanan?" asked Trowbridge interestedly.

"I don't remember his name, but it wasn't Buchanan then—at least, not in his home town. He must have just got out of the lock-up."

"I met the individual referred to yesterday—Pappy George Bilney introduced him to me. They 'peared to have struck up considerable of a friendship on the way down," the Sheriff said slowly. "I ain't seen this feller around the town to-day, neither. Prob'ly George told him all his secrets, too, on the way down. He never has learnt that there's bad men runnin' around the border. I've often thought of what a good chance fer a robbery George's emporium was, 'way off by itself thataway. By Godfrey, to-day's the first o' the month, too. I believe I'll mosey up to see George and Judy t'morrer." The Sheriff turned to Captain Perkins. "Cap'n, how about one o' the boys flyin' me up to Willett t'morrer? I shore am anxious to git up that way."

The commanding officer readily assented.

"Thanks, Cap'n," returned Trowbridge. "Sleepy, I ain't noticed you rushin' forward to offer yore services as chauffeur—"

"Oh, I'll be tickled pink," yawned Sleepy.

Helmet and goggles in hand, Sleepy, the next morning, made his way to the line, where a huge figure interestedly watched the efforts of the mechanics.

"Mornin'!" came the jovial hail of Trowbridge.

Sleepy nodded. The big twelve-cylinder Liberty increased its roar as the sergeant shoved the throttle wide open. The men, holding each wing and the tail, buckled to their work as the whirring propeller pulled the wheels against the blocks with seemingly irresistible force.

Slowly the drum of the mighty cylinders tapered off as the mechanics drew back the throttle. Spears adjusted helmet and goggles, and then helped in the Sheriff, who looked like an old eagle.

One of the mechanics saw to it that the belt was safely snapped around him while Sleepy took a look at his instruments from beneath drooping eyelids. The air-pressure was two and a half and the oil-pressure a safe thirty. Quick trials of each switch proved that both sets of plugs were working perfectly. Temperature 70 Centigrade, voltmeter charging, gasoline pet-cocks switched on the main tank, horizontal stabilizer at neutral—the maze of wheels and instruments and pet-cocks and pumps that filled the cock-pit made a connected story which his drowsy eyes read effortlessly.

He glanced back at the Sheriff, who filled the rear cock-pit to overflowing. The Sheriff waved a puffy arm to signify his readiness to depart.

At Sleepy's nod, the mechanics pulled the blocks from the wheels, and then swarmed at the edge of the left wing, holding it back while Sleepy turned the De Haviland around with full gun and left rudder on as far as it would go. Without stopping for a moment, he neutralized his rudder, shoved the stick forward, and in a moment was scudding across the field with accelerating speed. The pilot sat carelessly, his right arm draped restfully on the padded cowling that rimmed the cock-pit.

Without any reason at all, he gave the ship right rudder, and it swerved to the right; then left rudder, and a quick left turn was the result. In a moment the ground sank below them; then Sleepy banked carelessly, his lower wing barely three feet above the ground. Then a left bank, combined with a mild zoom, and the thirty-four-hundred-pound ship lifted over the hangars on the western edge of the field in a climbing turn, seeming literally to graze the sides, so close was it.

The pilot looked back with a slow grin, to see Sheriff Trowbridge holding to the cowling as if the force of his grip might make some difference.

"He flies too casual-like," was Trowbridge's judgment, before he lost himself in the joy of the rushing air. The flat, misty earth was now five hundred feet below them as they circled the airdrome.

Sleepy pulled back the throttle until the tachometer showed fifteen hundred revolutions a minute, and wheeled the stabilizer forward a trifle until the ship rode level. By means of the stabilizer a ship can be made nose or tail heavy by changing the angle of the two flat surfaces on the tail.

A quick glance at the many little glass-covered gauges before him showed that everything was all right. The ship rode the smooth, cool morning air buoyantly, and by the time it had made one circle of the field had reached a thousand feet. Sleepy threw it into a vertical bank, and in a moment the railroad was in sight, leading northward through the mesquit.

He hunched down farther in the seat, until the great motor ahead of him shut off all forward vision. His right arm rested limply on the cowling, and his feet were propped comfortably on the rudder-bar. The car-shattering roar of the Liberty was as soothing as a lullaby to his accustomed ears. He did not vouchsafe a glance at the receding ground below. He settled down for the forty-minute trip as if in an automobile.

Sheriff Trowbridge was in the seventh heaven. The billowing mesquit, fading into dim nothingness twenty miles away, the rush of the air, the speed with which familiar landmarks were picked up and left behind, all represented the greatest thrill the veteran had ever experienced in his variegated career.

The southeast wind blowing from the Gulf of Mexico was slightly stronger than usual, and in thirty-five minutes the Sheriff glimpsed the clearing that represented Willett. The sun had burned away the ground-mist, and each tiny tree and weather-stained railroad-tie stood out plainly in the clear golden air. He shook the stick in the back seat—the usual signal from cock-pit to cock-pit. Sleepy, who had been sitting as motionless as an image, did not immediately take cognizance of the signal. Not until the Sheriff had actually caused the ship to wabble with the force of his hand on the stick did the pilot turn his heavy-lidded eyes backward. Trowbridge unthinkingly threw out an arm to point. The combined force of the propeller blast and a hundred and twenty miles an hour of speed knocked it backward with painful suddenness; but Sleepy understood.

The tiny station and the store warehouses and corral, with the barely discernible road leading past the store and to the station, labeled their destination plainly. The clearing skirted the road on the south side, and appeared to be about four hundred yards long and a hundred yards wide.

Sleepy cut the motor to thirteen hundred and fifty revolutions, and as he nosed down, the speedometer jumped to a hundred and thirty-five miles an hour. In a shallow spiral he circled the field, dropping down to twenty-five hundred. Then he nosed upward and banked smoothly to the left, jamming on full right rudder as the big ship tilted. It shot downward on the tip of the left wing in a wicked side-slip.

Trowbridge grabbed his goggles to keep them from blowing sideways, and strove to get his breath and conquer that sinking sensation in his stomach. In a moment the nose dropped, and in a smooth wing-turn the ship zoomed upward again and banked to the right. Another side-slip to the right, and they were down to fifteen hundred feet.

With a somewhat strained smile twisting his lips, the Sheriff watched Sleepy handle his ship. The flyer's eyes rested steadily on the field below, and he seemed to fly instinctively. Alternately to the right and left, the roaring ship dropped downward. At five hundred feet Sleepy gave it full gun and flashed across the field for a last look. It appeared to be a close-cut hayfield, with no particular obstacle except a shallow ditch cutting diagonally across the northeast corner.

The ship swept out of the slip barely a foot above the ground, and sped across the ground with quickly decreasing speed. For a split-second it seemed to hover, and at the instant Sleepy jerked the stick back. Came the crunch of the tail skid and the rumble of the wheels on the ground in a perfect three-point landing. Most people do not know that alongside a perfect landing most of the thrilling acrobatic flying they "oh" and "ah" is child's play.

The big plane stopped rolling a hundred yards short of the end of the field, and Sleepy promptly turned off the gas pet-cock, to allow the motor to run itself out of gas. By this method damaging backfire in the expensive, fragile motor would be impossible. In a moment the Liberty sputtered and died, and the seven-foot propeller came to rest. He clicked off the switches and released the air-pressure.

"You use these things right careless-like," came the Sheriff's voice, vague because ear-drums were still humming from the roar of the motor.

The pilot unstrapped himself, climbed out, and leaned restfully against the trailing edge of a wing while he set fire to a cigarette and watched the Sheriff release himself from his belt and climb out.

"Funny there ain't nobody out to greet us," remarked Trowbridge. "Let's mosey over to the emporium." The front door was closed; and there was not a sign of life. They went to the back door, and the Sheriff knocked without result. He tried the door experimentally, and it opened.

"I don't quite get the lay," said Trowbridge, as he led Spears into the sitting-room. "O George! You lazy old counter-jumper, where be yuh?"

A muffled cry came to them from the store. Without a word, Trowbridge lumbered swiftly up the passageway that led to the store, Spears behind him.

"Great God!" breathed the Sheriff, as he reached the office door. Almost before the words were out of his mouth, Sleepy was peering over his shoulder at the gruesome tableau.

The body of Bilney he almost forgot for the moment, as he met the tearless, burning eyes of the girl, eery above the gag-bandage that covered her face. Trowbridge dropped to his knees beside the body of his friend. With a catlike leap, Spears hurdled the body and ripped at the girl's bonds. Her large eyes gave him the creeps—they seemed like the only part of her alive.

"He's still alive," said Trowbridge, with ominous calmness, as he arose. "Judy girl, what happened?"

For a moment the girl neither moved nor spoke. Sleepy stood quietly beside her, his narrowed eyes watching the girl unwinkingly, as cold as the glint of sunlight on ice.

Then, in lifeless tones, the girl told the story while Trowbridge gently wiped her father's wound with his bandana. As her story unfolded, her low-pitched voice grew louder. Suddenly the barriers of her artificial repression gave way. With a heart-rending cry, she threw herself on the body of her father. Her hands caressed his thin, blood-stained gray hair, and her lips were pressed to his withered cheek.

"I'm gittin' some water," said Trowbridge slowly, and disappeared.

Without speaking, Sleepy went into the store and caught up a blanket. He returned, and wrapped it round the girl in her torn nightgown. Then he put one arm under her and gently raised her to her feet as the Sheriff returned with a basin of water. Spears led the sobbing girl to a chair.

In silence broken only by the girl's weeping, Trowbridge washed and bound the wound. Then he slowly got to his feet, his mahogany face a mask from which two thin slits flashed wrath that was terrible in its all-consuming force.

"I'd die happy the minute after I'd shot the skunk that did this," he rasped, his face working suddenly.

"If you'll shoot as you never shot before, maybe you can get him," said Spears, the timbre of his voice subtly different. "Listen. This Buchanan would make for the border, wouldn't he?"

"Uh-huh."

"If it wasn't for leaving Miss Judith and her father here alone—"

The Sheriff comprehended the generalities of Spears's plan immediately. He whirled on Judith.

"Where's Cissy, Judy?" he asked.

"I—I don't know. She——"

Trowbridge plunged down the passageway. In a moment he returned, leading the half-dead old negress.

"Listen, Judy; you say you heard Buchanan take your horse?"

The girl nodded, her face hidden in her arms.

"Cissy, you take care o' Mr. Bilney. Judy girl, get yoreself together and ride Buchanan's horse to the nearest telephone. 'Phone the airdrome at McMullen, and tell 'em to send Doc Spurgin up here by ship to tend to yore daddy—I believe the doc can save him. Spears and I'll take after this coyote, and mebbe we can find him."

He looked at Spears, and for the first time noticed the change in him. Glowing eyes, body like a coiled spring—he gave an impression of leashed power waiting eagerly to be unbound.

"Let's be about it," he said briefly.

Together, as gently as possible, they lifted Mr. Bilney's unconscious form and carried it to his room.

"Git dressed and start, Judy; we'll see that the horse is ready," said the Sheriff. "We're on our way."

"Oh, I hope you get him!" the girl said passionately. She seemed ablaze as she stood there, a statue of vengeance personified.

The horse was in the corral, unsaddled. It was the work of a moment for the Sheriff to saddle him. Meanwhile Sleepy made for the ship with long strides.

He climbed into the cock-pit, and without a single lost motion turned on the gas, set the air-pump, and rapidly pumped up the air to three pounds. This done, he adjusted the priming pet-cock and sent three stiff shots of gasoline into the cylinders. As Trowbridge came lumbering across the field, Sleepy was twirling the propeller. The effortless ease with which he overcame the compression of the big motor and the weight of the heavy stick would have been an eye-opener to some of Spears's best friends.

"Ready, son?" bellowed Trowbridge.

"Just about. Here's the scheme. He'll probably stay pretty close to the railroad in order to keep a straight course for the border, won't he?"

The puffing representative of the law nodded.

"Keep a close watch. If we spot him, I'll go low and stall the ship. When it hovers for a minute, shoot. I believe you can hit. It'll be ticklish work, Sheriff. I may not be able to catch the ship again after the stall."

"What do I care?" Trowbridge burst forth.

"I didn't think you would. How can we make sure when we've found our man?" asked Spears.

"I'd know Judy's pony anywhere," declared the old man truculently.

Without another word, Sleepy went back to the cock-pit and snapped on the switches.

"I'll pull you—I'm more used to this cranking than you are."

As the Sheriff set himself with one hand on the prop, Spears grasped his other wrist with both of his hands. In time to the count, the two men swung backward and forward, without moving the propeller until "Three!"

With all his strength, Spears jerked the Sheriff away from the stick. The huge body actually left the ground under the power of the pilot's pull. The Liberty caught, and Spears leaped for the cock-pit to advance the spark and throttle until there was no danger of the motor dying.

Trowbridge removed his cover-alls, literally tearing them off in his haste. His inseparable companions, the two big six-shooters, came into view, their pearl butts protruding from the swinging holsters. By the time Spears had strapped himself in and had begun to run the motor up in a quick warm-up, his passenger was ready.

When the temperature-gauge showed 60 Centigrade, the flyer glanced back. The Sheriff was standing up, peering at the instruments over his shoulder. For a second two pairs of gleaming eyes met in wordless appraisal. To the old man the devil that danced behind the cold sheen of the pilot's eyes meant many things. In that moment was born an understanding which went deeper than mutual participation in the coming venture—it was a revealment of the fundamentals in the younger man's make-up.

Without a word Spears turned and gave the De Haviland the gun. It skidded around in a close circle, and then with the ever-increasing roar of the Liberty sped across the field on its mission.

At two thousand feet they had a clear radius of vision of ten miles. The tachometer showed seventeen hundred revolutions a minute as with wide-open motor the ship drove toward the border at a hundred and twenty miles an hour. Ceaselessly two pairs of eyes searched the far-flung desert of mesquit below, striving to spot the figure of a horseman.

Spears figured that, provided Judith's estimate of time was correct, Buchanan would have covered about forty miles. She thought that the crime had been committed about one o'clock. He was flying a few miles west of the railroad, in the belief that his prey would strike a straight course for the border. With all his heart the grim-faced pilot hoped that they might find him. Time after time the tableau in the barren little office arose before his eyes, momentarily blotting out the flat green panorama below. With every fiber of him he craved personal vengeance—the opportunity to wreak punishment on the man who had left a girl bound and gagged to watch over her all but dead father.

Twenty minutes out, both men redoubled the minute care with which they searched the ground, which was like a painted curtain half a mile below. It was Trowbridge who suddenly grasped the stick and rocked the ship back and forth exultantly.

Spears turned and his eyes followed the Sheriff's pointing finger. Sure enough, there was a mounted man crossing a tiny clearing, two or three miles to the westward. Without cutting his motor, Spears nosed down.

Struts vibrated madly, and wires shrilled to the terrific speed of the ship as it darted earthward. Little by little, Spears shot downward in a tight spiral, the pivot point of which was the now galloping figure below. Like some prehistoric monster circling for a kill, the De Haviland roared earthward.

Little by little, Spears shot downward
toward the galloping figure below

As he reduced the motor revolutions to a thousand, Spears frequently jazzed the throttle to keep the spark-plugs from fouling with oil. In a moment he would need every bit of the Liberty's four hundred and fifty horsepower—and need it without a second's delay on the motor's part.

At two hundred feet, half a mile back of Buchanan, who was now invisible, Spears shoved the throttle wide open. The motor sputtered a moment, and then caught. The ship hurtled across the mesquit like a drab brown comet. The sensation of speed so close to the ground was tremendous. In a few seconds they flashed across a wildly galloping horse carrying a man whose upturned face was a smudge of white.

Spears, hunched down behind the wind shield, turned his head and glanced inquiringly at his passenger. Trowbridge nodded violently.

Spears banked so suddenly that it threw the Sheriff against the side of his cock-pit. The De Haviland swept around to the left, mushing slightly because of its terrific speed. Sleepy kept it nosed down until it was scraping the tops of the mesquit trees as he straightened out once more.

A hundred yards back of the fleeing Buchanan, he cut the gun. The ship swept on with decreasing speed. A few yards behind the man on the ground, its speed was seventy-five miles an hour. Trowbridge, fighting the wind-blast, was standing up, both guns in his hands.

Then Sleepy took his chance. He nosed up, banking to the right at the same time. For a second the airplane hovered, right wing down, above its prey. Each of Trowbridge's guns spoke twice. Like a flash, Sleepy rammed the throttle full on, glimpsing the fall of the horse below out of the corner of his eyes.

The fouled plugs did not catch immediately, and the infinitesimal delay was fatal. The ship, being so low and having lost flying speed, could not stay in the air any longer, and there was not altitude enough to pull out. In that split-second Sleepy had an opportunity, however, to do what he had planned all along if he did not win his gamble—for he had never planned that the grizzled old-timer in the back seat should take his full share of the flying chances.

Banked as it was, full top rudder would have dashed the ship into the ground on its side, and the Sheriff would have borne the brunt of the crash. Instead, Sleepy shoved the stick forward as far as it would go. With his arm thrown in front of his face, he rammed the ship into the ground. Wings sheered off on trees, and then came a stupendous crash that marked the cessation of consciousness for the pilot.

Trowbridge, stunned as his head was dashed against the front cowling of the cock-pit, found himself lying on his side in the middle of a twisted mass that represented the broken fuselage. He struggled weakly, and then sank back with a groan. Apparently his collar-bone was broken, and his right arm for some reason would not function.

He fumbled at the belt dazedly, and succeeded in freeing himself. Bit by bit, he crawled out of the débris, looking around for Spears. As he dragged himself out, the spat of a revolver sounded, and the whine of a bullet past his head made him duck so suddenly that he nearly fainted with the pain.

He peered toward the place where the shot had apparently come from, shielded from sight by the wreckage. Fifty yards away was the carcass of the dead horse, and even as he looked a man's head lifted itself above the body. Trowbridge snaked his way the few inches to the remains of the cock-pit, and was rewarded with a shot that drilled through the débris just beside him. He found one of his guns, jammed between two twisted longerons. As his groping hand grasped it, a searing pain in his left leg seemed to come simultaneously with the crack of another shot.

It was a moment before his will proved superior to the physical weakness that all but overpowered him. Then he started to crawl, with infinite pains, the foot necessary to reach a point of vantage. Through the twisted wreckage he peered with bloodshot eyes, his sixshooter in his left hand.

In two minutes he was rewarded. Once again Buchanan's head protruded slightly from his barricade. Trowbridge sighted, this time, his gun resting on a piece of shattered ash. With all the remnants of his strength, he forced himself to be careful. When the gun spoke, Buchanan's head dropped limply on the horse.

Trowbridge's right arm was wounded. With infinite pains, he crawled out, his revolver in his left hand.

It took the Sheriff two hours to bind the flesh wound in his leg and release Spears. The pilot was lying half under the motor, which had been jammed part way through the fuselage, leaving barely a foot of clearance between itself and the back of the pilot's seat. One of Spears's legs was caught under it, and an unnaturally bent arm told its own story. Trowbridge did not succeed in bringing him back to consciousness before he himself tumbled over in the blazing heat of the Texas sun. Above, three vultures hovered curiously.

At ten-thirty in the morning, when no word had come of the ship's safe arrival at Willett, every plane at McMullen, except the two on patrol, was ordered out on the search. Jimmy Jennings found the wreck. From that time on, a ship was constantly hovering over the spot to guide the ground party. It was ten o'clock at night when Tex MacDowell's De Haviland, equipped with wing-lights, brought the rescue expedition to the crash. The men were brought back to McMullen on a special engine and caboose furnished by the little jerkwater railroad.

Spears came to briefly at the start of the trip, and did not wake up again until the next afternoon, when he found himself in the McMullen hospital, with Sheriff Trowbridge—none of whose bones had been broken—sitting beside his bed, and Captain Perkins standing at the foot. In a moment Major Searles, the flight surgeon, came in with the hospital physician.

"Welcome back," grinned the Sheriff.

"Glad to be here," returned Sleepy weakly. "Doc, what's ailing me?"

"Three broken ribs, a broken leg, and compound fracture of the right arm," replied the hospital man briskly. "We can fix you up as good as new."

"Outside of that, I'm all right, eh?" yawned the pilot "Did you get Buchanan, Sheriff?"

"In two parts," stated the Sheriff. "Polished off the job after we landed. Bilney is comin' along O.K. He and Judith are over to my house. She says she's aimin' to be an assistant nurse for you soon's her daddy gets better."

Sleepy's square face lightened with a slow smile.

"What's a few broken arms and legs compared to that prospect?" he queried gently. His eyelids dropped farther, and in a moment he was asleep again. The four men tiptoed out. Trowbridge stopped at the door and looked back on the tousled hair and tranquil face of the flyer.

"I think I'll get to understand a lot of things better down here if the border continues like this," said the commanding officer.

The Sheriff closed the door gently.

"Well," he drawled, "it is a fine place to git a valuation on real hombres."